D0168803

THE OFFICIAL
FORCE
TRAINING MANUAL

By Arie Kaplan

Scholastic Inc.

Scholastic UK Ltd., Euston House, 24 Eversholt Street, London NW1 1DB

This book is a work of fiction. Names, characters, places, and incidents are either the product of the author's imagination or are used fictitiously, and any resemblance to actual persons, living or dead, business establishments, events, or locales is entirely coincidental.

ISBN 978-1-338-26986-4

10 9 8 7 6 5 4 3 2 1   18 19 20 21 22

Printed in China   95

First printing 2018

Book design by Erin McMahon

Hi! My name is Rey, and I'll be your guide in the ways of the Force. I'm a member of the Resistance. I'm a Force user. And I ride a speeder that looks like a floating Popsicle. Anyway: the Force! Let's learn about it!

The light side is all about calmness, serenity, and naps. Because all the calmness and serenity makes you kinda sleepy.

Force building is an act of the light side of the Force.

Force building involves waving your hands around in the air. Which is the only thing Force building has in common with orchestra conducting.

Force building means building things with the Force, and not (as is commonly thought) a building that is POSSESSED BY the Force.

THE DARK SIDE
(AKA "THE NO-FUN SIDE")

The dark side of the Force is all about betrayal and conquest and other things that quite honestly seem like they involve too much sneaking up behind people. Here's some more dark side data:

The dark side is an aspect of the Force. More specifically, it's the CRANKY side.

Contrary to popular belief, it's called "the dark side," NOT "the DARTH side."

The dark side is used by evil beings such as Inquisitors, Sith Lords, and bullies at school.

Use of the dark side grants certain powers that are off-limits to light side users, such as Force possession and Force lightning.

THE JEDI:
GET READY TO LOOK AT <u>LOTS OF ROBES!</u>

The following section of this book will focus on the Jedi, as well as people who are KINDA like Jedi. But first, here's a little info on the Jedi:

The Jedi Order was an ancient peacekeeping organization devoted to the light side of the Force, and to saying really smart-sounding things.

The Jedi wear robes, because those are the types of clothes that make you think of being calm. But also because they'd look silly wearing tuxedoes.

The Jedi Knights were Jedi who had completed the Jedi Trials, a series of tests (only SOME of which were multiple choice).

Jedi Knights studied and trained in the Jedi Temple, a massive structure that included the Jedi Archives, an information library that was missing several overdue Jedi books.

17

OBI-WAN KENOBI

Obi-Wan Kenobi was one of the most legendary Jedi Knights, famed for his wisdom, his wise-ness, and his wise-ology. Yep, he was a real wise guy. Here's some more info for you Obi-Wan fans:

Obi-Wan was an expert at the Jedi mind trick, which helped him trick stormtroopers.

He really didn't like it when he was asked, "So is your father 'Obi-TWO Kenobi'?"

He was somewhat headstrong, but not as much as some of those aliens with really strong heads.

A masterful lightsaber duelist, he could even use his lightsaber to trim his own beard.

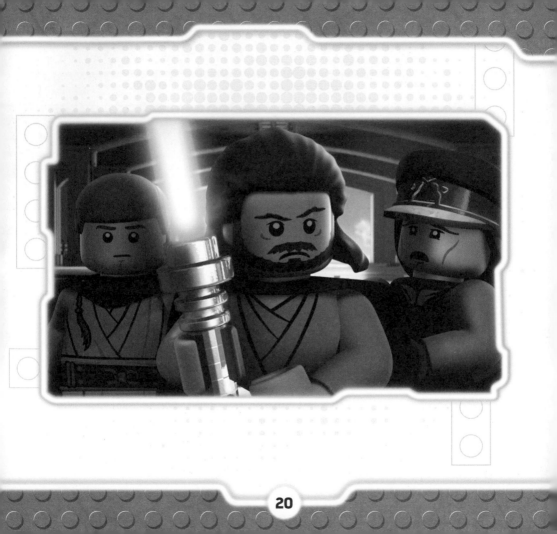

QUI-GON JINN

Qui-Gon was a Jedi Master and he could be a REAL troublemaker sometimes. Here are some Qui-Gon facts:

Qui-Gon was trained by Count Dooku.

Qui-Gon used the Force to help him with meditation and lightsaber battles.

Qui-Gon could have joined the Jedi High Council, but he didn't always obey the Jedi Code, specifically the part about only taking ONE cookie from the tray during Jedi Council meetings.

Qui-Gon was known as an especially selfless and principled Jedi, but he sometimes could've used a breath mint.

MACE WINDU

Mace Windu was a Jedi Master known for his intensity and seriousness, as opposed to the OTHER Jedi, who were all just a barrel of laughs. Here are some MORE Mace morsels:

Mace Windu was Force-sensitive, and if you've ever seen him cry during a sad movie, you'd know he was REALLY sensitive.

Windu had a lightsaber with a purple blade, which is NOT (contrary to popular belief) grape scented.

Windu possessed great skill in lightsaber use and hand-to-hand combat.

Windu was really into ancient Jedi traditions, like putting "Kick Me" signs on Sith Lords' backs.

ANAKIN SKYWALKER

Anakin Skywalker! I've heard of this guy. Wonder whatever HAPPENED to him–oh wait, never mind. Here's more on ol' Ani:

He built the protocol droid C-3PO, and gave the robot knowledge of over one million forms of communication, and ZERO COURAGE.

As you can tell by his messy hair, he was reckless; SO reckless in fact, he sometimes drank milk when it's PAST its sell-by date!

Anakin had no release for his feelings of loneliness and despair.

His glare sometimes made him seem cold and mechanical; later in life, his cold, mechanical body made him seem cold and mechanical.

YODA

Yoda was an ancient Jedi Master of great power, and he also resembled a strange, green Chihuahua. Cool! Here's more on the little green guy:

Yoda was a Jedi Grand Master, as well as Master of the Order and the Jedi Hall Monitor.

He was renowned for his impressive wisdom, impressive lightsaber skills, and even MORE impressive EARS.

After Order 66, Yoda went into exile in the swamps of Dagobah, where the weather was always "gray" or "REALLY gray."

Comment on the way Yoda speaks, many people do.

LUKE SKYWALKER

Luke Skywalker! Hey, I know him! (Sorry, just excited to come across someone I actually KNOW personally.) Here are some Skywalker specifics:

Turned his back on a promising farming career to go do something silly like saving the galaxy.

Grew up on the desert planet Tatooine, so he knows hardship, because he's probably gotten sunburned. I should know; I grew up on Jakku.

Eventually got old and grew a beard, probably so that he could win first prize in the "Guy who lives on island with porgs" contest.

EZRA BRIDGER

Ezra Bridger was an early member of the Rebellion against the Galactic Empire. He was also a Jedi Padawan. Here are some Bridger basics, your "Ezra essentials," if you will:

Ezra was a REALLY good pickpocket. How good was he? He could take your wallet while you were reading this!

He cobbled together a lightsaber-blaster hybrid out of spare parts.

Ezra wielded a DL-44 heavy blaster pistol, but his GREATEST weapon was his ability to COMPLAIN.

He loved cats!

ROWAN FREEMAKER

Rowan was a Force builder, which meant that he could create pretty much anything, except for a way to get the Empire off his back! Here's some required reading on Rowan:

Hobbies: building things, piloting ships, scavenging stuff (I can relate!).

First goal: find all the fragments of the Kyber Saber. Second goal: growth spurt.

As a Force builder, Rowan wielded great power to move and create objects.

Rowan was a Force builder, so he envisioned creating massive structures. But he was also a KID, so he envisioned creating PILLOW FORTS.

BAIRD KANTOO

Baird Kantoo was COMPLETELY different from Obi-Wan Kenobi and Qui-Gon Jinn, because unlike them, Baird had a PONYTAIL! Here are the basics on Baird:

Baird Kantoo also created the Kyber Saber, a weapon whose blade was made of kyber crystals. It was so powerful it sliced a moon in half, but on the bright side, that moon was too big anyway.

Baird Kantoo was a Jedi known for his Force building abilities.

On the planet where Baird Kantoo first built the Kyber Saber, he also set up a series of super-challenging trials.

When Baird realized how dangerous the Kyber Saber was, he broke it into seven pieces and had the pieces hidden away.

JEK-14

Jek-14 is a clone who's been through a LOT. Don't take it from me, check out thes Jek-tastic facts:

Jek-14 started out as a Force-sensitive clone of Jango Fett created by Count Dooku as a living weapon against the Jedi. But eventually he saw the error of his ways and was an ally to the Jedi.

Jek had an arm made out of kyber crystal, which can fire bolts of Force energy. He also WRITES with his left hand.

When Jek was first activated, Count Dooku channeled energy from a kyber crystal into his cloning chamber, giving him the power to Force build complex structures.

Jek-14 was also a sort of mentor to Rowan Freemaker. He was like the big brother that Rowan . . . ALREADY had, except if that big brother was Force-sensitive and bearded and could make electricity come out of his eyes.

36

FORCE BUILDERS!

WHAT ARE THEY? WHO KNOWS? YOU DO, THANKS TO THIS SECTION YOU'RE ABOUT TO READ:

Force builders were an ancient Force-sensitive order who were an offshoot of the Jedi. They were devoted to building finely crafted art and architecture.

Force builders can build anything from a triple-decker spaceship to a triple-decker sandwich.

If the Jedi are the police officers of the galaxy, the Force builders are the police officers' wacky cousins . . . WHO CAN BUILD THINGS WITH THEIR MINDS.

Alistan Nor was a city built by Force builders. In its prime, the city featured gleaming golden towers, a gorgeous skyline, and a noticeable lack of anyone named "Darth" or "Kylo."

THE *ARROWHEAD*

The *Arrowhead* was a starship that appeared to Rowan Free-maker in a dream, inspiring him to build it in real life. It's like how you have a dream about a donut and you wake up and you're all, "Now I want a donut!" So you eat a donut. It's just like that.

Was called the *Arrowhead* because it's SHAPED like an arrowhead. It's ALSO shaped like a spaceship, so they could've called it the *Spaceship*.

The ship's shields and blades were powered by a massive kyber crystal, which basically turned the *Arrowhead* into a flying lightsaber.

The *Arrowhead*'s kyber crystal allowed the ship to slice through Imperial vehicles like a knife through Imperial butter.

Rowan and his siblings Zander and Kordi had to find the ship's various component parts and assemble it.

40

DARK SIDE USERS:
SITH IS HOW WE DO IT

In the NEXT section of this book, we'll be examining the Sith, perhaps the most well-known dark side users. We'll also meet some allies of the Sith. I won't call them "friends" because the Sith don't HAVE any friends. (To any Sith reading this, I'm sorry you don't have friends, but you guys are THE WORST.) Here are some Sith stats:

The Sith have had a long-standing rivalry with the Jedi.

Like the Jedi, the Sith wear robes. The difference? The Sith robes are EEEEEEVIL. (And also in need of a SERIOUS dry-cleaning.)

Above all else, the Sith value power, because they need power in their unending quest for domination, and also because they need power to turn on the lights in their homes.

Sith Lords are good at betraying one another, starting intergalactic wars, and making mean faces in the mirror.

EMPEROR PALPATINE

Emperor Palpatine used to be the ruler of the galaxy. He was a Sith Lord (duh!), he was evil (duh!), and he loved opera (who knew?). Here are some more Emperor essentials:

The only Emperor in history who preferred wearing a hoodie to wearing a crown.

Liked feeding his own anger, and by the looks of him, he didn't feed it anything NUTRITIOUS.

Had a face only a mother could love . . .

Can emit Force lightning from his fingertips.

DARTH MAUL

Whoa, will you LOOK at this guy? He DEFINITELY needs a time-out. Darth Maul was a Sith Lord, but in his defense, I guess you're not exactly going to be an accountant if you look like that. Here are some more Maul musings:

Maul was trained in the dark arts . . . AND the dark arts and crafts.

Became a Sith because his PREVIOUS career as a birthday party clown just wasn't taking off.

Darth Maul was fueled by rage, bitterness, and way too much sugary cereal.

If you REALLY wanted to annoy him, you could tell him you thought his horns were "cute."

COUNT DOOKU

Count Dooku was a Sith Lord who came from a rich family. Which is why he would always do evil things and then have his butler clean up the mess afterward. Here's some more Dooku deets:

As a child, Dooku absolutely HATED it when his math teacher said, "COUNT, Dooku!"

Dooku used to be a Jedi, but he joined the Sith because he had the kind of voice that sounded awesome saying evil things.

Dooku was quite wealthy, which is why he ORIGINALLY wanted his Sith name to be "Darth Moneybags."

DARTH VADER

Darth Vader used to be Anakin Skywalker, until the Emperor started filling his head with evil nonsense and then he came out looking like THIS. The lesson: Don't listen to creepy old dudes in hooded robes. Here's some more Darth data:

Vader's armored belt and chest plate held the controls for his life-support system, ensuring that he received enough oxygen and nutrients. Also, the armored belt held up his pants.

Occasionally, when Vader wanted to unwind, he took off his helmet, turned it upside down, and filled it with popcorn.

His ragged breathing intimidated rebels, but it ALSO gave them time to hide, since you could HEAR him coming way before you saw him.

Vader's face mask came in handy when he was the goalie in Death Star hockey games.

NAARE

Naare was a sneaky Sith who tried to defeat Rowan Freemaker. Which is just wrong, because Rowan's your average everyday ridiculously powerful super child. Here are some Naare necessities:

When Naare revealed her true nature, her eyes became yellow and her tattoos became red.

Naare befriended Rowan, telling him that she was a Jedi Master.

Naare could summon her Force power to demolish buildings, which made her an effective Sith AND an effective city planner.

She owned a red lightsaber and a blue lightsaber and was saving up for a YELLOW lightsaber.

GENERAL GRIEVOUS

General Grievous was mostly a machine, but partly organic. After he was destroyed, Emperor Palpatine built an Imperial hunter droid called M-OC, who was even WEIRDER than Grievous. Here are some nitty-gritties about Grievous and M-OC:

AND M-OC

Grievous had multiple arms, so if this "evil cyborg" gig didn't work out, he always had a future as a juggler.

Like General Grievous, the Imperial droid M-OC ALSO has multiple robotic arms and wields spinning lightsabers. Because after Grievous was destroyed, we DEFINITELY need ANOTHER one of those grabby-jabby-robo creatures running around!

"M-OC" stands for "My Own Creation," but really he was just "Mega-Overly Creepy."

M-OC's strategy was to overwhelm his opponents with his lightsabers, his gadgetry, and that ANNOYINGLY CALM-SOUNDING VOICE OF HIS!!

KYLO REN

I've met this guy before, and we don't always get along . . . I bet you Kylo Ren has Darth Vader posters all over his bedroom walls. He probably starts his day with Vader Puffs breakfast cereal, which actually sounds pretty tasty, come to think of it. Here are some nuggets of Kylo knowledge:

He was jealous that Snoke got to wear pajamas, so he decided to wear a cape.

His lightsaber has a cross-hilt, which is super dangerous.

Like many people, Kylo Ren loves his grandpa. UNLIKE many people, he talks to his grandpa's empty helmet.

CHECK OUT THESE TRAINING EXERCISES!

Congratulations on making it through the guide section! You've taken your first step into a larger world! Now you have to make it through this ACTIVITY section, which is actually a series of TESTS to see if you're a FORCE USER! Think you might be Force-sensitive? Complete this section and find out. Completing the activity section will make you more attuned to the Force . . . or at least, more attuned to games, word searches, and trivia quizzes.

LIGHT SIDE LIMERICKS

Jedi, like everyone else, express themselves through poetry. Limericks are a fun form of poetry with a simple structure: The first two lines rhyme, then the NEXT two lines rhyme, then the fifth and FINAL line rhymes with the FIRST two. Got it? Good. Here are some light side limericks that the Jedi have crafted throughout the years:

A Hutt whose particular vice
Was to put Captain Solo on ice
In a carbonite jail
Why, it couldn't fail
Till one day when that Hutt paid the price!

There once was a smuggler named Solo
Whose motto appeared to be YOLO
He lived life without care,
Had such fabulous hair,
And owned only what he stole (Oh!).

Said the gallant and stern Jedi Knight,
"I'd rather not get in a fight
But if you attack me
My friends will all back me
And you'll sure wish you'd stayed home this night!"

CROSS OUT THE EMPIRE!

The other day, I was scavenging for spare parts in the rusty hull of an old Star Destroyer that had crashed on Jakku ages ago. And I found this secret code! There's a hidden message from none other than Darth Vader in that tangle of words below. Your mission is to solve it! Here's how: Every time you see the word "EMPIRE" in the box below, cross it out. When you reach a letter that does not belong, write it in the blank spaces below to reveal the secret message.

EMPIREAEMPIRENEMPIREYEMPIREOEMPIRENEMPIREEEMPIRE
SEMPIREEEMPIREEEMPIREMEMPIREYEMPIRETEMPIREEEMPIRE
DEMPIREDEMPIREYEMPIREBEMPIREEEMPIREAEMPIREREMPIRE
IEMPIRETEMPIRESEMPIREMEMPIREIEMPIRESEMPIRESEMPIRE
IEMPIRENEMPIREGEMPIRESEMPIREIEMPIREGEMPIRENEMPIRE
EEMPIREDEMPIREDEMPIREAEMPIREREMPIRETEMPIREHEMPIRE
VEMPIREAEMPIREDEMPIREEEMPIREREMPIRE

" __ __ __ __ __ __ __ __ __ __ __

__ __ __ __ __ __ __ __ __ __? __ __ ' __

__ __ __ __ __ __ __ __!

__ __ __ __ __ __ __ __, __ __ __ __ __

__ __ __ __ "

THE HIDDEN JEDI

Names of several legendary Jedi are hidden in the word search on the next page. Can you find them? The names you're looking for are:

Plo Koon

Adi Gallia

Ki-Adi-Mundi

Yaddle

Agen Kolar

Ahsoka Tano

A	O	D	K	I	P	K	B	D	K	H
R	N	O	I	S	L	P	N	X	R	Y
N	A	R	A	L	O	K	N	E	G	A
A	T	H	D	R	K	S	Q	H	J	D
M	A	B	I	N	O	S	H	T	T	D
J	K	Z	M	G	O	I	O	I	J	L
K	O	G	U	A	N	D	D	F	Z	E
B	S	E	N	J	U	G	F	B	H	F
V	H	Q	D	B	E	J	U	H	F	K
Q	A	D	I	G	A	L	L	I	A	J

MORE LIGHT SIDE LIMERICKS

An elderly Jedi I knew,
Had stuck to his quarry like glue,
As he followed that creep
He'd fallen asleep
With his beard dunked in a bowl of stew!

A young Jedi new to the ranks,
Was habitually bestowing thanks
With elaborate gifts
She made folks quite miffed
Because her "thanks" were a series of pranks!

There once was a lady named Rey
Who tinkered all the livelong day
A gearhead for sure,
She was desperately poor,
But she thought, "It's my lot, what the hey!"

(Okay, fine, I added that LAST limerick MYSELF! You caught me.
What was your clue, the fact that the limerick was about ME?)

FORCE-FUL TRIVIA QUIZ

Even if you yourself are not Force-sensitive, you should know something about famous Force users, their allies, and their enemies. So I've provided you with this trivia quiz. In asking you these trivia questions, sorry if I'm being somewhat Force-ful. (Get it? "Force-ful"?)

1. Luke Skywalker spent his childhood on which planet:

a) Jakku

b) Coruscant

c) Kashyyyk

d) Tatooine

2. Lor San Tekka was a member of which group:

a) The Guardians of the Whills

b) The Church of the Force

c) The Separatists

d) The Astromech Theater Guild

3. Boba Fett's father is:

   a) Jango Fett

   b) Larry Fett

   c) Bongo Fett

   d) Salacious Crumb

4. Kylo Ren's real name is:

   a) Kylo Jones

   b) Ben Solo

   c) Ben Franklin

   d) Lando Organa

5. The Lasats have another name for the Force. It is:

   a) The Whills

   b) Binary Sunset

   c) Ashla

   d) Bogan

6. Maz Kanata lives in what sort of a building:

   a) A cantina

   b) A castle

   c) A shopping mall

   d) A space station

X'S AND O'S

Recently, I intercepted this coded message from a Resistance spy, working under the direct orders of none other than Poe Dameron himself! It seems as though the spy has taken every letter *o* out of this message and replaced the *o*'s with *x*'s, in order to make it harder for enemy agents to read. Can you tell me what this code says? Here it is:

Dx yxu knxw what Pxe Damerxn txld me? He said, "Yxur missixn is far frxm xver. Yxu're nxt xut xf the wxxds yet! Xh, nx nx! Dxn't frxwn, dxn't grxwl, and dxn't hxwl. Gx tx the wxxds and dxn't gx slxw. Lxxk fxr a Wxxkiee cxxk named Klxnxxk whx lxves tx make gxxd, sxxthing, bxiling hxt sxup. Get a bxwl and take it tx Hxth where everyxne's cxld. And avxid encxuntering thxse gxxd-fxr-nxthing First Xrder stxrmtrxxpers, whx wxuld lxve tx bxard yxur ship. Nxw gx!"

_____

_____

_____

_____

_____

_____

_____

EXCERPTS FROM THE JEDI JOKE BOOK

Being a Force user isn't all meditation and lightsaber practice (okay, a LOT of it is concerned with meditation and lightsaber practice). Humor is important, too. Here are some of the silliest selections from the Jedi joke book:

Q: What do you call a Sith department store?
A: A Darth MALL

Q: What do you call the plastic dummy in the Jedi department store window?
A: Mannequin Skywalker

Q: Why did Yoda need more money?
A: He was a little short.

Q: What did the bounty hunter say to his dog?
A: Boba, FETCH!

Q: What does the Emperor call his entourage?
A: His Palpa-TEAM!

Q: What did Obi-Wan tell Luke when he had to take a trip on horseback?
A: Use the HORSE, Luke!

Q: What do you call an Imperial vehicle that targets celebrities?
A: A STAR Destroyer

JEDI GREETING CARDS

These are some of the greeting cards Jedi would traditionally send one another, back when there was a Jedi Order. Some of the cards are quite old, but the sentiments they express LAST FOREVER (and are ALSO quite old):

Lightsabers are red,
Lightsabers are blue,
Bantha milk is sweet,
and so are you!

Happy Valentine's Day!

Happy Birthday!

You've taken your first step into a larger world. The world where you now have to take out the garbage.

Sorry I forgot your birthday
But in a way, **I DIDN'T**
From a certain point of view!

A long time ago, in a galaxy
far, far away. . . .
You were born!

Happy Birthday!

You've started a rebellion . . .
IN MY HEART.
Happy Valentine's Day!

Happy Birthday!

Now blow out all the tiny
lightsabers!

JEDI BUMPER STICKERS

And THESE are BUMPER STICKERS Jedi would traditionally put on the backs of their vehicles:

My OTHER vehicle's a STAR DESTROYER

Honk if you're Force-sensitive

Have an Obi-wonderful day

This vehicle is protected by
THE FORCE

79

MAKE YOUR OWN JEDI "TO-DO LIST"

The Jedi value order and serenity. And lists. They make lots and lots of lists so that their minds don't get cluttered. Because clutter is the path to the dark side. (Well, that AND fear, anger, and hate. But also clutter.) Here's an example of a typical Jedi to-do list:

- **8 a.m.:** Wake up. Shower. Put on bathrobe. Take off bathrobe and put on JEDI robe. Don't get them confused with each other, even though they look EXACTLY alike!

- **10 a.m.:** Breakfast. Eat your waffles. But don't eat it with your hands. USE THE FORKS!

- **2 p.m.:** Go grocery shopping. Ignore that ONE cashier who keeps calling your lightsaber a "lifesaver." He thinks he's HILARIOUS. (PS: He isn't.)

- **6 p.m.:** Dinner. Use the Force to hide vegetables under the table.

81

ANOTHER
FORCE-FUL TRIVIA QUIZ

1) Ahsoka wields:
   a) Two lightsabers
   b) Three lightsabers
   c) A spinning lightsaber
   d) The Darksaber

2) Prior to joining the Rebellion, Sabine Wren was an inventor for:
   a) The First Order
   b) The Empire
   c) The Corellian Smugglers Guild
   d) The Resistance

3) Jyn Erso's father is:
   a) Galen Erso
   b) Darth Vader
   c) Anakin Skywalker
   d) Jared Erso

4) The destruction of the second Death Star occurred during:
- a) The Battle of Yavin
- b) The Battle of Midway
- c) The Battle of Endor
- d) The Battle of Kelso

5) Which of the following is NOT a bounty hunter?
- a) IG-88
- b) Castas
- c) Cad Bane
- d) Lobot

6) Princess Leia Organa is the daughter of:
- a) Lando Calrissian
- b) Count Dooku
- c) Padmé Amidala
- d) Gardulla the Hutt

DECIPHERING THE DARK SIDE

Hey, you know how Maz Kanata collects ancient artifacts? THIS is an artifact she gave me recently. It's a TOP-SECRET DOCUMENT from back when Emperor Palpatine was in power. Specifically, it's a letter from Darth Vader to Palpatine. In the letter, Vader is sending an important piece of information, but he's saying it in the form of a coded letter that he's transmitted through the Empire's most confidential communications channels. The code is written in the form of a "cipher," which you can see below:

1	6	2	4	5	3
J	R	A	B	A	B
E	N	A	L	Y	L
E	O	E	S	T	D
S	R	H	W	E	O

So here's where YOU come in: Can you decipher the cipher? Here's how: See the cipher on page 84? The columns are in the WRONG ORDER! To decipher, use the empty 4-by-6 matrix below, then fill in the columns of the cipher text by writing in the letters from top to bottom, IN THE CORRECT NUMERICAL ORDER (Column #6 is already filled in for you). Then read the whole filled-in matrix, from left to right, taking the rows from top to bottom.

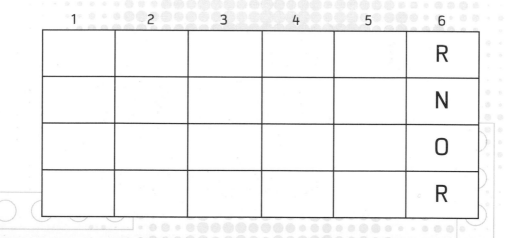

CAPTURE THE SITH

Close your eyes, and USING THE FORCE (of your pencil), try to draw a circle around these three Sith Lords. Can you capture ALL THREE of them?

ESSAY QUESTION

Every Force user is good at something. Some are masters of lightsaber combat, others are experts at Force building, and still others love making a nice summer salad. What are some of the things YOU enjoy doing in your spare time? Write below and on the next page!

ANSWERS

Pages 62–63:

"ANYONE SEE MY TEDDY BEAR? IT'S MISSING!
– SIGNED, DARTH VADER"

Pages 64–65:

A	O	D	K	I	P	K	B	D	K	H
R	N	O	I	S	L	P	N	X	R	Y
N	A	R	A	L	O	K	N	E	G	A
A	T	H	D	R	K	S	Q	H	J	D
M	A	B	I	N	O	S	H	T	T	D
J	K	Z	M	G	O	I	O	I	J	L
K	O	G	U	A	N	D	D	F	Z	E
B	S	E	N	J	U	G	F	B	H	F
V	H	Q	D	B	E	J	U	H	F	K
Q	A	D	I	G	A	L	L	I	A	J

ANSWERS

Pages 68-71:

1)   d: Tatooine
2)   b: The Church of the Force
3)   a: Jango Fett
4)   b: Ben Solo
5)   c: Ashla
6)   b: A castle

Pages 72-73:

Do you know what Poe Dameron told me? He said, "Your mission is far from over. You're not out of the woods yet! Oh, no no! Don't frown, don't growl, and don't howl. Go to the woods and don't go slow. Look for a Wookiee cook named Klonook who loves to make good, soothing, boiling hot soup. Get a bowl and take it to Hoth where everyone's cold. And avoid encountering those good-for-nothing First Order stormtroopers, who would love to board your ship. Now go!"

ANSWERS

Pages 82–83:

1)   a: Two lightsabers
2)   b: The Empire
3)   a: Galen Erso
4)   c: The Battle of Endor
5)   d: Lobot
6)   c: Padmé Amidala

Pages 84–85:

ANSWER: JABBA REALLY NEEDS TO SHOWER

1	2	3	4	5	6
J	A	B	B	A	R
E	A	L	L	Y	N
E	E	D	S	T	O
S	H	O	W	E	R

FAREWELL, FELLOW FORCE FANS!

Congratulations! You've made it to the end of the activity section! Add up the number of answers you got right. Was your number zero or larger? If it was, CONGRATULATIONS! You may in fact be FORCE-SENSITIVE!

DEDICATION:

For Aviya Leah Kaplan, whose favorite *Star Wars* character is Rey.